/VERLASSEN/

by Avery Lewis

/VERLASSEN/

/VERLASSEN/
German: To Leave; Abandon.

VERLASSEN by Avery Lewis was workshopped and developed at Augusta University and premiered at the Maxwell Performing Arts Theatre, located at 2500 Walton Way, Augusta, GA in May 2023. It was directed by Avery Lewis with set design by Doug Joiner. Music composed by Alex Thomas. Stage managed by Kelyisha Hayden. The cast was as follows:

JAMES .... Noah Bowers
MATTHEW .... Jamal Bogan
PASTOR EMMETT .... Caroline Holt
IDA .... Wednesday Ayabarreno
MRS. VERLASSEN .... Alina Bacal
BOOKIE .... Jaysen Lami
BOXKEEPER .... St. Julian Cox III
TOWNSPERSON .... Destiny Barrett
TOWNSPERSON .... Kayla Johnson
TOWNSPERSON .... Tyler Millwood
TOWNSPERSON .... Brihanna Lewin
TOWNSPERSON .... Makaelyn Martin

/ VERLASSEN /

CHARACTERS

JAMES VERLASSEN
Middle-aged man, condemned to be executed.

DRUNK
Middle-aged man, former teacher, current alcoholic.

IDA
Teenage daughter of James.

PASTOR EMMETT
Pastor and subsequent leader of the town.

MRS. VERLASSEN
Middle-aged woman, Ida's mother.

BOXKEEPER
Man or woman of any adult age, the keeper of the names.

TOWNSPEOPLE, BOOKIES, CONGREGANTS, GUARDS
Various ensemble roles.

PLACE
A small town.

TIME
Morning to noon.

NOTES

The lines for ensemble roles (*Townspeople, Bookies, Congregants, and Guards*) are designed to be played by multiple cast members. The town can be made up of a big ensemble or a small ensemble. Feel free to assign these lines to various actors in the ensemble based on the size of your cast.

When taking on James' execution in the final scene, it is important to note that an actual guillotine is not necessary. Directors are free to be as literal or abstract as they choose to be. Creative liberty is encouraged.

When coming upon an ellipsis in the script (…) this indicates a nonverbal response to the previous line. The way the ellipsis is acted is left up to the actor and director, but it should not go unacknowledged.

When coming upon a slash in the script, this indicates an interruption. The next character with a line should begin their line when the slash appears.

NOTE ON MUSIC

The song sung in Scene 4, "Bright Morning Stars", is a traditional Appalachian spiritual song in the public domain.

SCENE 1

"SHE'S WEARING YELLOW TODAY"

---

*At rise, James and the Drunk are sitting face to face,
only separated by prison bars. James is on the inside
of the cell; the Drunk on the outside. It's quiet for a
while. The Drunk is already drinking, but not yet
drunk.*

JAMES. How is she?

DRUNK. Which one?

JAMES. …

DRUNK. …

JAMES. …

DRUNK. She's wearing yellow today.

JAMES. Does she know?

DRUNK. No. Do you want her to know?

JAMES. No.

DRUNK. Her mother is -

JAMES. Don't.

DRUNK. She doesn't know either. The town never knows.
It's all part of the show.

JAMES. Funny to think this all ends in a show.

DRUNK. You always were able to put on a good act, James.

JAMES. Not always.

DRUNK. Well, it was good enough to get my patrol killed.

May as well have killed me.

JAMES. You're alive.

DRUNK. I'm a ghost.

JAMES. A ghost that -

DRUNK. Haunts.

JAMES. Why?

DRUNK. Because you're my ghost as well. You're a constant reminder of who I used to be. I'm haunted everyday you're alive.

JAMES. Well you won't have to deal with that much longer, huh?

DRUNK. I'm sure you'll find a way to keep at it long after you're gone. *(James laughs.)* I brought you something for today. *(He takes a bottle of whiskey from his coat and passes it to James through the bars.)*

JAMES. You know I don't drink.

DRUNK. Who doesn't drink on a day like today?

JAMES. I don't drink.

DRUNK. "Give strong drink unto him that is ready to perish, and wine unto those that be of heavy hearts. Let him drink, and forget his poverty, and remember his misery no more."

JAMES. So you're a saint now?

DRUNK. Not a saint, just a student.

JAMES. The teacher becomes a student, huh?

DRUNK. The teacher should always be a student.

JAMES. Very well.

DRUNK. I miss it sometimes.

JAMES. Teaching?

DRUNK. Teaching. Believing. Living. I haven't always been like this.

JAMES. I know. I remember.

DRUNK. I was an honorable man.

JAMES. You still can be.

DRUNK. You took that from me. You took everything from me.

JAMES. …

DRUNK. …

JAMES. …

DRUNK. You know you deserve to die for what you did.

JAMES. I know more than anyone.

DRUNK. Because who could possibly know more than James Verlassen?

JAMES. That's not what I meant.

DRUNK. We thought you were one of us. I had to spend three months watching my men die off. One by one. I taught some of them. They were just boys. They were just boys fighting a grown man's war. And look where that got them. Betrayed and killed. You know, somehow, you're luckier than those boys. You get a quick and clean way out. Those boys had to suffer. They had to wake up every morning not knowing if it would be their last day. Wake up maybe even hoping it would be their last day. You remember Henry? Henry didn't want to starve anymore. He fed on false hope more than bread. He ended up taking his own life so he wouldn't have to suffer the same fate as his friends. John had to slave away in the cold only to be shot when he stopped working. Every day, when Joseph, William, and Arthur were brought into the shower, they had no way of knowing if they were getting cleaned or if they were getting gassed. Hell, to this day I get nervous to even walk into a shower. Because every time I do, I can hear their muffled screams. My breath catches every time the water comes on because I half expect to die. How are your showers? You put them through that, and you get the easy way out. (He laughs and takes a long drink.) Son of bitch. After all of these years, I can't do it. I just can't bring myself to forgive you. Because forgiving you would mean forgetting what it looked like when that bullet tore through John's skull. Or the way William looked at me when he realized you betrayed us. He trusted you more than anything, James. You were like a father to him. And Henry. The image of Henry's body is branded in my mind. So I drink. I guess that means forgiving you would mean putting down the bottle for good. But this bottle… it's become a part of me.

JAMES. …

DRUNK. …

JAMES. So, she's wearing yellow?

DRUNK. It seems so.

JAMES. Yellow. You'd think she knows.

DRUNK. What do you mean?

JAMES. I just imagined that if she knew, she would be glad.

DRUNK. Whether she knows or not, there's a bigger issue at hand.

JAMES. And what would that be?

DRUNK. Why is she wearing yellow? *(James is speechless, unsure how to answer his question. Drunk lets out a burst of sudden laughter.)*

JAMES. What?

DRUNK. Your daughter has your eyes, you know.

JAMES. I've never seen -

DRUNK. She has your vacancy. Your ghosts. She has no laughter in her eyes.

JAMES. I guess that would be my fault. She grew up without a father.

DRUNK. She grew up with her father's ghosts.

JAMES. Are you sure she doesn't know?

DRUNK. No one knows, James.

JAMES. How can you be sure?

DRUNK. If people knew, your family would be here with you.

JAMES. Maybe it would be nice to have people with me.

DRUNK. You want your family to be imprisoned with you?

JAMES. That's not what I meant.

DRUNK. It's what you said.

JAMES. I meant … it becomes lonely very fast here. It would be nice to have someone here.

DRUNK. When have you been one to need a friend?

JAMES. You'd be surprised. *(From offstage a buzzer can be heard indicating that the visiting hour is over.)*

DRUNK. Memento vivere, Lieutenant.

JAMES. Look after her, please.

DRUNK. That's what I've been doing. *(He begins to exit.)*

JAMES. Thank you for being my friend.

DRUNK. *(Beat.)* All my friends are dead. *(Drunk exits leaving James alone in his cell. After a moment, James reaches and grabs the bottle and cracks the seal.)*

    End of scene.

SCENE 2

*"YOU MAY NOT EVEN REMEMBER ME …
BUT MY LAST WORDS WILL BE FOR YOU"*

In the town square, the energy is overwhelming. Townspeople are drinking gleefully, A pair of Bookies are taking bets, and a religious group sings hymns of praise and celebration. There's clapping, laughing, dancing, and shouting.

BOOKIE ONE. Place your bets here! Place your bets here! Take your chance to win big!

BOOKIE TWO. Will it work? How many tries will it take? Take your bets and place them here!

BOOKIE ONE. Guillotine? Noose? Firing squad?

BOOKIE TWO. Electrocution? Stoning? Suffocation?

TOWNSPEOPLE. *(Several townspeople say the following lines.)* … No more stonings! It's become a bore!

… Bring back the rats! It makes it last longer.

… Or the electric chair. That was a good year.

… I've heard that this time they're gonna use the firing squad.

… I've heard that it's a woman getting executed. They wouldn't use a firing squad on a lady.

… If she's being executed, she ain't no lady! *(They all howl in laughter.)*

… I'll wager two coins for a woman being executed by a firing squad!

… Put me down for the same bet, sirs!

BOOKIE ONE. *(Rings a bell to get the crowd's attention.)* First bets placed!

ALL. First bets placed! *(Townspeople all cheer.)*

BOOKIE ONE. The first bet will be two coins wagered for a woman executed by firing squad!

BOOKIE TWO. Will it work? How many tries will it take? Take your bets and place them here! *(A Townswoman who had been singing hymns dances over to where the Bookies are taking bets.)*

TOWNSWOMAN. I think they'll be hung. And I think it'll be instant. No suffering.

BOOKIE ONE. *(Laughs.)* No suffering!

BOOKIE TWO. Lady, have you seen a hanging before?

TOWNSWOMAN. If their soul is saved there will be no reason for suffering.

BOOKIE TWO. Your wager?

TOWNSWOMAN. I'll wager ten coins.

BOOKIE ONE. Ten coins! Ten coins wagered for hanging without suffering! Place your bets here!

BOOKIE TWO. Will it work? How many tries will it take? Take your bets and place them here! *(The pair of Bookies move away from the center of town square, making way for Pastor Emmett and his Congregation to come forward.)*

CONGREGANT ONE. Aren't you going to place a bet, Pastor?

PASTOR EMMETT. I always keep my bets to myself.

CONGREGANT ONE. Why?

PASTOR EMMETT. I'd hate to ruin the fun for anyone else.

CONGREGANT TWO. *(In awe.)* So you know?

PASTOR EMMETT. I can't say that I know for sure. But I pray long and hard for days like today. My prayers usually seem to grant me more … wisdom.

CONGREGANT TWO. Oh, tell us Pastor, what will it be?

CONGREGANT ONE. Do you know who will be chosen?

PASTOR EMMETT. *(Chuckling.)* Lean not on what I say, for I am just human.

CONGREGANT ONE. *(Looking at the clock tower.)* It's almost time!

CONGREGANT TWO. It's almost time!

PASTOR EMMETT. *(Projecting his voice for all to hear.)* Come. Let us rejoice. For today we are blessed to witness one of life's greatest moments. The saving of a soul. And the departure of that soul to meet its savior. For many years we have seen condemned individuals rebuke their past ways. Murderers, traitors, and thieves have repented right before our eyes. And moments later, they enter into their eternal home. This is all thanks to each and every one of you. Your dedication and faith throughout the years is why heaven will be full. Brothers and sisters, this is our chance to minister to a lost soul. May we seize this opportunity. And may we treat every day like it is execution day. *(The bell tower chimes.)* It is now time to select who will have the honor of being Executioner. May they serve us with pride. Can the box keeper come forth? *(The Boxkeeper approaches Pastor Emmett with a large wooden box and holds it out in front of him.)* Do you swear that you have performed your annual responsibility of conducting the town census?

BOXKEEPER. I do.

PASTOR EMMETT. Do you swear that you have handwritten the name of each citizen over the age of thirteen on its own paper?

BOXKEEPER. I do.

PASTOR EMMETT. And do you swear that since the collection and writing of those names that you have prayed over each of them individually?

BOXKEEPER. I do.

PASTOR EMMETT. Thank you for your service to this town. Let us pray. *(Pastor Emmett bows his head, leading the rest of the Townspeople to do the same. They all say the following prayer in unison.)* Our Father who art in Heaven, hallowed be thy name. Thy Kingdom come; Thy will be done on earth as it is in heaven. Give us this day our daily bread and forgive us our trespasses as we punish those who trespass against us. And lead us not into temptation but deliver us from evil. For Thine is the kingdom, the power, and the glory. Forever and ever. Amen. *(By himself.)* Lord of mercy and grace, be with us this day. Make yourself known to the one condemned today. May your peace be with them as they take their final breath today. And may your peace be with us as we lead each other closer to you. Forever. Amen.

TOWNSPEOPLE: Amen.

PASTOR EMMETT. It is time. *(He reaches his hand into the box and pulls out a slip of paper. There is a hush in the crowd as the Townspeople wait in suspense.)* This year's town Executioner will be … *(He opens the slip of paper and reads the name.)* Ida Verlassen. *(The town breaks into cheers. They make a path for Ida to walk through. Her pale, yellow dress stands out amongst the sea of townspeople dressed in dull colors. Her mother, Mrs. Verlassen, is walking by her side, beaming.)*

> *Vignette. Everyone freezes in place. There is a lighting transition to James as he enters. In his shackled hands, he clutches the bottle of whiskey he was previously given by the Drunk.*

JAMES. I don't remember my father. I'm often glad I don't.

Times like today I wish I could. Every now and then I'll think about him though. I'll try to imagine what he would be like. Then I'll ask myself things like, do I have his laugh? Do we have the same drink? *(He takes a swig.)* Sometimes I think I remember my mother. But that can't be her. She died in childbirth. She was just a kid. So was dad. Not much older than you. When mom died, he didn't want to be a father anymore. So he gave me up. To The Guard. Thought they would have a better chance of raising me right. He left me with nothing. Not even a name. The Guard thought it would be funny to call me Verlassen. The name James came later. Looking back I guess it is pretty funny. Calling the abandoned boy Verlassen. Little baby Verlassen. That name is all I gave to you, and now look. I've abandoned you too. It's funny how life works like that. *(Beat.)* Do you remember me, Ida? Do you remember how I would rock you back to sleep when you would wake up crying? Or the lullaby I would sing to you? *(To himself.)* "Bright morning stars are rising, Bright morning stars are rising. Day is a breaking in my soul." Those are my favorite memories. They're what finally gave my life meaning. *(The clock tower rings; with sudden panic.)* I need you to remember something other than what you're about to see today. When the Executioner asks me for my last words, I'll find you in the crowd. He said you're wearing yellow, so you should be easy to find. You may not recognize me. You may not even remember me. But my last words will be for you. *(He exits.)*

> *End Vignette. Lighting transitions back to the town as everyone picks up where they left off. Ida makes her way through the path of Townspeople alongside her mother. The cheering continues.*

PASTOR EMMETT. Congratulations, dear girl. You must be so proud, Mrs. Verlassen.

MRS. VERLASSEN. I am.

PASTOR EMMETT. Well, Congratulations to you as well.

This is a great honor for your whole family.

MRS. VERLASSEN. Thank you, Pastor. We're truly honored to have this opportunity.

PASTOR EMMETT. I'm sure you are. However, what comes next is just for Ida. *(To the crowd.)* I'm taking our Executioner to meet the condemned. Continue your celebration!

MRS. VERLASSEN. Pastor, are you sure I shouldn't be there with her?

PASTOR EMMETT. Mrs. Verlassen, this is the way it's always done. Only Ida and myself can have communication with the condemned.

MRS. VERLASSEN. Yes, Pastor.

PASTOR EMMET: I'll bring her back shortly. Come, Ida, we have a long walk ahead of us.

    End of scene.

SCENE 3

"LOVE MAKES US DESIRE JUSTICE"

Ida and Pastor Emmett walk in silence for a moment. Ida suddenly stops.

PASTOR EMMETT. Is everything alright, Ida?

IDA. Forgive me if I sound rude, Pastor, but … I feel like this must be some sort of mistake.

PASTOR EMMETT. There are no mistakes, Ida.

IDA. It's strange. This is only the third year my name has ever been in the drawing. There are so many others who would love to have this chance. Yet I'm the one chosen. I don't feel right about this.

PASTOR EMMETT. We must not lean on our feelings. They are deceptive. They're ever changing. If you follow where your feelings go, you'll be walking in circles for the rest of your life. What is all of this, Ida?

IDA. Can I be honest?

PASTOR EMMETT. Always.

IDA. I've never understood Execution Day. Why do we celebrate it? Why do we have to have an execution at all?

PASTOR EMMETT. "An eye for an eye, tooth for tooth, hand for hand, foot for foot, burn for burn, wound for wound, and bruise for bruise."

IDA. I don't understand.

PASTOR EMMETT. Do you want children one day, Ida?

IDA. *(Caught off guard.)* I've always wanted a son. To honor my father. Why do you ask?

PASTOR EMMETT. The love a parent has for a child is unlike any other. And love makes us desire justice. You clearly already love this little boy, and right now he's only a figment of your imagination. Your love for James will teach you more than you can imagine. If someone were to hurt that boy, you would want justice. I can promise you, your mother feels that same way about you. I feel the same for my children. All because of love. Love is the reason we have execution day. Every time someone is executed, justice is served and love is satisfied. That is why we celebrate.

IDA. I thought we celebrated because we're saving souls.

PASTOR EMMETT. We celebrate that as well. Some have a celebratory drink for justice. Some have a drink for the soul. And others just … drink.

 IDA. What do you drink to, Pastor?

PASTOR EMMETT. *(Ponders a moment.)* As a pastor, I should say I drink for the soul. *(He laughs.)* Is this all making sense now?

IDA. It is.

PASTOR EMMETT. These aren't innocent people we're executing. He deserves his punishment.

IDA. …

PASTOR EMMETT. *(Catching himself.)* That's why we work so hard to save their souls. Otherwise, they'd be damned.

IDA. Did you know my father?

PASTOR EMMETT. …

IDA. I never said his name. But you knew I would want to name my son James.

PASTOR EMMETT. Ida, as a pastor, I have come to know

most people in our town.

IDA. So you did know him.

PASTOR EMMET: I married him and your mother. They had me baptize you as a child. Yes I knew him, but I never personally knew him.

IDA. Oh.

PASTOR EMMETT. I've done the same for just about every other person in our town.

IDA. I was just hoping that … I barely remember him. I only have just a few vague memories. Mom doesn't talk about him anymore. I've never known my grandparents. I have no connection to him. I guess I was hoping that you could help me.

PASTOR EMMETT. I'm sorry, Ida. *(Observes a moment.)* You have his eyes.

IDA. I do?

PASTOR EMMETT. You do.

IDA. Thank you, Pastor.

PASTOR EMMETT. Your soul is still burdened. What is it?

IDA. I understand why we execute now. I do. But I don't think I can be Executioner. It doesn't feel right.

PASTOR EMMETT. We must not lean -

IDA. On our feelings, I know. I know. But there's just something about the thought of it. I couldn't live with myself. I've spent my entire life hating The Guard. The people who stole my father's life. How could I hold onto those feelings if I also take a life? There must be another way, Pastor.

PASTOR EMMETT. Ida, you have been chosen.

IDA. But why can't another name be chosen?

PASTOR EMMETT. How about we make a deal?

IDA. What is it?

PASTOR EMMETT. Wait until you meet the condemned before you make up your mind. Don't throw away this opportunity before you fully understand it. *(Ida ponders his offer. Silence fills the rest of their walk as they approach the prison.)* After you.

End of scene.

SCENE 4

---

*"I'M GOING TO TAKE PLEASURE IN SEEING YOUR
DAUGHTER KILL YOU"*

---

*Ida and Pastor Emmett are now in the prison, where
a drunken James is sitting with his back facing the
pair. Ida enters first followed by Pastor Emmett.*

PASTOR EMMETT. The Executioner is here to meet you.

JAMES. *(Slurring his words.)* I don't care to see anyone.

PASTOR EMMETT. This is how it's done.

JAMES. *(Angrily, he confronts Pastor Emmett.)* I said I -
*(He notices the yellow dress on Ida; overwhelmed with
emotion.)* No.

IDA. Is he drunk?

PASTOR EMMET: They usually are.

IDA. What is he in here for?

PASTOR EMMETT. You've learned about the Great War,
haven't you?

IDA. Of course.

PASTOR EMMETT. During the war, our town had a patrol.
Mostly full of young boys. Not all, but mostly. Sixteen,
seventeen years old. They went to fight in the war to
maintain the purity of our land. Little did they know the
leader of their patrol was a mole. You see Ida, they had been
planning an uprising. The day they were going to attack,
they were ambushed by The Guard. Their plans were
airtight They knew one of their own had to be a rat. They

were all taken prisoner. Thrown in a camp. No one survived. Not a single one of them. *(Regarding James.)* This was the man. His betrayal cost mothers their sons. Sisters their brothers. Daughters their fathers. He cost me -

IDA. I'll do it.

PASTOR EMMET: What?

IDA. I'll be Executioner.

PASTOR EMMETT. You will?

IDA. Yes. You were right. These aren't innocent people. These are the same people who killed my father. He deserves to die.

PASTOR EMMETT. I'm glad you've come around.

IDA. Why did he do it?

PASTOR EMMETT. It's been hard to get him to talk. We've had him here for years. We still don't know why.

IDA. *(To James.)* Why did you do it?

PASTOR EMMETT. *(Growing annoyed.)* Ida, he isn't going to talk.

JAMES. *(Overwhelmed with emotion.)* I'm sorry. I'm sorry. I'm so sorry.

IDA. Why?

PASTOR EMMETT. Ida, stop.

JAMES. I'm sorry. I'm sorry. I'm -

IDA. Why did you kill my father?!

PASTOR EMMETT. Ida -

JAMES. For you. I did it for you. Forgive me, Ida. *(James reaches a hand through the bars to her. His fingers barely brush the yellow dress.)* Forgive me.

PASTOR EMMETT. *(Pulling Ida away from James.)* That's enough!

JAMES. *(Together.)* Wait!

IDA. *(Together.)* How does he know -?

PASTOR EMMETT. *(Losing composure.)* That's enough! *(James and Ida fall silent.)* Ida, return home.

IDA. No.

PASTOR EMMETT. Now is not the time.

JAMES. Ida …

IDA. Who is this man?!

JAMES. Ida …

PASTOR EMMETT. Go back to town with your mother.

IDA. *(To James.)* How do you know me?

JAMES. Ida …

PASTOR EMMETT. Go.

IDA. I still have questions.

PASTOR EMMETT. Now is not the time.

IDA. I've been waiting for answers my whole life. When will it be time?

PASTOR EMMETT. When I return to town.

IDA …

PASTOR EMMETT. Goodbye, Ida. *(Ida lingers a little longer, then slowly exits.)*

JAMES. I've lost everything.

PASTOR EMMETT. You've lost everything? How can you possibly say you've lost everything? Your daughter is still alive.

JAMES. *(To himself.)* She's going to kill me.

PASTOR EMMETT. Just like you killed my son.

JAMES. …

PASTOR EMMETT. Do you remember Henry?

JAMES. …

PASTOR EMMETT. Do you remember any of them?

JAMES. …

PASTOR EMMETT. You know, I still remember the day

my wife and I got that knock on our door. When we opened it, I saw two uniformed men standing there. They told us that Henry had been captured. Taken to a prison camp. But at least that meant there was still hope. Hope that someday, he could come home. Alive. When the war ended and they went to liberate the prison camp, I knew that any day, my son would be coming home. That's when those two uniformed men showed back up. There were no survivors. All of that hope I had been holding onto … gone. Just like my son. For so long, my wife and I lived without answers. She eventually succumbed to her grief. But God has a way of making things right. Doesn't he, James? I was told that a member of The Guard had been captured and sentenced to execution. The same member who was the double agent. The ringleader. The man who betrayed my son. I was asked to come pray with the prisoner. You can only imagine my surprise when I walked in and saw you, of all people, sitting there in shackles. So now you're going to tell me. What happened to Henry? How did he die?

JAMES. I wasn't at the camp when he died.

PASTOR EMMETT. Do you really want to go to your death with this on your conscience?

JAMES. *(Laughs.)* Let's not pretend to care about my conscience, Pastor.

PASTOR EMMETT. I'll ask you one more time. What happened to my son?

JAMES. No.

PASTOR EMMETT. No?!

JAMES. You don't want to know.

PASTOR EMMETT. You don't get to tell me what I don't want to know. What happened to my son?

JAMES. …

PASTOR EMMETT. Tell me!

JAMES. *(Quietly; with shame.)* He killed himself.

PASTOR EMMETT. …

JAMES. He didn't want to suffer anymore. So he ended his life on his terms.

PASTOR EMMETT. Don't lie to me, James.

JAMES. I wish I was.

PASTOR EMMETT. My son would never give up like that.

JAMES. He had no fight left in him.

PASTOR EMMETT. …

JAMES. …

PASTOR EMMETT. …

JAMES. …

PASTOR EMMETT. I don't believe you.

JAMES. You don't have to believe me. You can take Henry's words for it.

PASTOR EMMETT. …

JAMES. He left a note.

PASTOR EMMETT. What did it say?

JAMES. Read it for yourself.

PASTOR EMMETT. …

JAMES. Matthew has it.

PASTOR EMMETT. Matthew died.

JAMES. He visited me today.

PASTOR EMMETT. There were no survivors. Matthew is dead.

JAMES. He's very much alive. He's been the only visitor I've had since I've been here.

PASTOR EMMETT. You're a mad man. No one knows you're here. No one knows you're alive. And Matthew, along with my son, has been dead. For ten years. All you do is lie. Lie, lie, lie. Do you know where liars go, James? Hell. They all go to hell. *(A moment of silence passes. Pastor*

Emmett is livid.) You know, I'm going to take pleasure in seeing your daughter kill you.

JAMES. You're really going to let her go through with it?

PASTOR EMMETT. You heard her as well as I did. She wants to.

JAMES. You're a sick man, Emmett.

PASTOR EMMETT. I'd rather be sick than depraved. I'll see you at noon, Verlassen. *(He begins to leave.)*

JAMES. Wait! *(Pastor Emmett stops but doesn't turn around.)* I've accepted my death. I deserve it. Please, just leave Ida out of this.

PASTOR EMMETT. I find her inclusion quite fitting.

JAMES. *(Pleading.)* For Ida. Not me.

PASTOR EMMETT. Goodbye, James.

JAMES. Wait! Wait! *(Pastor Emmett exits as James tries to fight his way through the bars.)*

    End of scene.

SCENE 5

"DAY IS A BREAKING IN MY SOUL"

James is alone in his cell. He's drunk and weeping. A stray Townsperson enters the stage with a guitar and sits on a bench near the prison. They begin to play. A look of recognition crosses James' face. It's the lullaby he would sing to Ida.

TOWNSPERSON: *(Singing.)*
BRIGHT MORNING STARS ARE RISING
BRIGHT MORNING STARS ARE RISING
BRIGHT MORNING STARS ARE RISING
DAY IS A BREAKING IN MY SOUL

WHERE ARE OUR DEAR MOTHERS
THEY ARE SINGING TO THEIR BABIES
THEY ARE SINGING TO THEIR BABIES
DAY IS A BREAKING IN MY SOUL

THEY HAVE GONE TO HEAVEN SHOUTING
THEY HAVE GONE TO HEAVEN SHOUTING
THEY HAVE GONE TO HEAVEN SHOUTING
DAY IS A BREAKING IN MY SOUL

Ida enters the stage, making her way back home. She stops in her tracks when she hears the song. She stands still for a moment. She begins to quietly sing along.

WHERE ARE OUR DEAR FATHERS
THEY ARE SINGING TO THEIR BABIES
THEY ARE SINGING TO THEIR BABIES

DAY IS A BREAKING IN MY SOUL

> *As the townsperson continues to play, Ida's emotions overwhelm her. She approaches the Townsperson and leaves a single coin by their side. A tip for the beautiful lullaby. During this, a guard takes James out of his prison cell, leaving just the Townsperson onstage.*

BRIGHT MORNING STARS ARE RISING
BRIGHT MORNING STARS ARE RISING
BRIGHT MORNING STARS ARE RISING
DAY IS A BREAKING IN MY SOUL

> *The Townsperson rises, collecting their coin, and exits, strumming and whistling along.*

> *End of scene.*

SCENE 6

"THE SKY WAS AN HOURGLASS. EACH STAR A GRAIN OF SAND, COUNTING AWAY MY TIME"

In the town square, Townspeople are congratulating Mrs. Verlassen. All of them drinking, singing, and placing bets as they do so. The Drunk stands close to Mrs. Verlassen reciting lines from the Book of Sirach.

DRUNK. "Weep for the dead, for he lacks the light; and weep for the fool, for he lacks intelligence" *(Mrs. Verlassen smiles politely, but doesn't respond.)* "Weep less bitterly for the dead, for he has attained rest /But the life of the fool is worse than death."

MRS. VERLASSEN. *(With familiarity, she says the next phrase in unison with the Drunk.)* /"But the life of the fool is worse than death."

DRUNK. The book of Sirach. Not many people are familiar with it. Fewer can finish a quote. Today's a fitting occasion.

MRS. VERLASSEN. Do you ever wonder about the condemned? Were they fools? Should we pity them?

DRUNK. …

MRS. VERLASSEN. I've never been any good at making those kinds of judgments. Who am I to say what kind of person someone else is, or was … or intended to be?

DRUNK. If a person is awaiting death, I don't think our judgment is what they're most worried about.

MRS. VERLASSEN. I once knew someone who was

fascinated with Sirach and other ... *(With caution.)* ... similar texts. You remind me of him.

DRUNK. James?

MRS. VERLASSEN. You knew James?

DRUNK. Quite well actually. *(Considers.)* At least, I thought I did.

MRS. VERLASSEN. How did you know him?

DRUNK. Work.

MRS. VERLASSEN. My husband never talked much about work.

DRUNK. I don't see a wedding ring.

MRS.VERLASSEN. I stopped. Wearing his ring. Recently. He ... he died ten years ago.

DRUNK. Did he?

MRS. VERLASSEN. I'm sorry, this is a terrible way to find out about a friend's death -

DRUNK. All my friends are dead. James is no friend of mine.

MRS. VERLASSEN. ...

DRUNK. I still remember the last time I saw James in uniform. I, along with the other survivors of my Patrol, were being loaded into a train car to be shipped away to prison. For some reason my commander, James Verlassen, wasn't with us. He was outside of the train car. His uniform was different. It was one of deep red with gold embellishments. The uniform of the enemy. I caught his eye while he was shaking hands with the General of The Guard, our enemy. I'll never forget that look. He knew what was going to happen to us, yet there was nothing in his eyes. They were vacant.

MRS. VERLASSEN. ...

DRUNK. Mrs. Verlassen, how well did you know your husband?

MRS. VERLASSEN. He was my husband.

DRUNK. Did you know that he was a member of The Guard?

MRS. VERLASSEN. …

DRUNK. Did you know that he's been alive for the past ten years?

MRS. VERLASSEN. If he was alive, he would be here. With me and my daughter. He loved us.

DRUNK. Did he love you?

MRS. VERLASSEN. …

DRUNK. Did he trust you?

MRS. VERLASSEN. … *(She's breaking.)*

DRUNK. *(He presses her further.)* Did h-

MRS. VERLASSEN. Stop. Please.

DRUNK. No.

MRS. VERLASSEN. You don't know what you're talking about. My husband died fighting The Guard. He died an honorable death.

DRUNK. He did no such thing.

MRS. VERLASSEN. Why are you doing this?

DRUNK. Because a young girl's innocence is at stake.

MRS. VERLASSEN. Leave my daughter out of this.

DRUNK. I came back to this town a couple years ago. It was an Execution Day, actually. I saw this young lady in a yellow dress. I thought, how odd, to wear yellow. What an odd choice of color to wear to such an event. A yellow flag of joy in a sea of grays and whites. That's when I saw her eyes. I recognized James in those eyes. They were the same eyes that sent me to what should have been my death. It was Ida. I wanted to say something. But even if my legs would have taken me to her, my mouth refused to speak. For the first time in my life, words abandoned me. She was so happy in that yellow dress. Innocence radiated from her. I've been keeping an eye on her ever since. She wears the same dress to every execution, she's not hard to miss. I made it my job to protect her from the truth. She thinks her father died a hero. It would destroy her if she knew who he really was. What he really did. That kind of devastation is the killer of joy. And now Ida has been chosen to be the killer of James unless you do something about it.

MRS. VERLASSEN. …

DRUNK. Mrs. Verlassen -

MRS. VERLASSEN. Would you just … give me a moment. Please.

DRUNK. You don't have a moment. At twelve o'clock, James will be carted out here to be executed. By your daughter.

MRS. VERLASSEN. Stop it. Just stop it. I'm losing my husband all over again. And now I have to figure out how to tell all of this to Ida?

DRUNK. *(Softens.)* I'm sorry.

MRS. VERLASSEN. You should be.

DRUNK. …

MRS. VERLASSEN. We were happy, you know. Me and Ida. I did the work to grieve James, to move on, and to make a good life for my daughter. And we were happy.

DRUNK. …

MRS. VERLASSEN. I can't do anything about this.

DRUNK. …

MRS. VERLASSEN. Ida's chosen. Her name was drawn. This town doesn't stray from its traditions. And my family has to pay the price for that.

DRUNK. You want your daughter to kill your husband?

MRS. VERLASSEN. Of course I don't.

DRUNK. Ida is only fifteen. She's still a child. The town

charter clearly states that if a citizen is drawn to be Executioner, and they have not yet achieved adulthood, the legal guardian of that citizen has the right to withdraw their name.

MRS. VERLASSEN. …

DRUNK. Withdraw her name. There's a way out of this for your family.

MRS. VERLASSEN. Pastor Emmett will never allow it.

DRUNK. That's why we need to draw another name now. Before the Pastor comes back. *(Mrs. Verlassen takes that in and then, after a moment, she walks to the center of town square.)*

MRS. VERLASSEN. Excuse me. *(She can barely be heard above the noise of celebration.)* EXCUSE ME! *(The town falls silent. Everyone looks to her.)* Our town charter states that the legal guardian of a minor can withdraw the minor's name if they are chosen to be Executioner. Therefore, I am withdrawing Ida's name as Executioner and will be selecting a replacement. *(There is chatter amongst the crowd.)* Could the Box Keeper bring me the names?

BOXKEEPER. *(He brings her the box and then whispers.)* Are you sure this is what you want to do?

MRS. VERLASSEN. I'm certain.

BOXKEEPER. May God bless you.

MRS. VERLASSEN. *(She reaches her hand into the box and picks a slip of paper. The town is in a hushed suspense.)* The new Executioner will be … *(She opens the paper. Her face falls.)* This can't be right.

BOXKEEPER. What does it say?

MRS. VERLASSEN. It's Ida. Again. *(Drunk comes over and observes the paper himself. He's shocked.)*

BOXKEEPER. Perhaps her paper was placed back in the box. Draw another.

MRS. VERLASSEN. *(She reaches back in the box and pulls out another slip of paper. She reads it.)* It's Ida. This paper says Ida. *(She grabs a handful of papers out of the box. She opens one. And another. And another. It's Ida. It's Ida. It's Ida.)* They're all Ida. Every one of them says Ida. *(To the Boxkeeper.)* What did you do?

BOXKEEPER. What?

MRS. VERLASSEN. Every paper I've opened has my daughter's name on it. What did you do?

BOXKEEPER. I took the town census and wrote down 1,500 different names.

MRS. VERLASSEN. Then how did every paper in this box get my daughter's name on it?

BOXKEEPER. You haven't opened every paper. *(Mrs. Verlassen takes the box from the Boxkeeper and shakes all of the papers onto the ground. She and Drunk scramble to read them all.)*

MRS. VERLASSEN. Ida. Ida. Ida. Ida. Every one of them says Ida.

BOXKEEPER. I had nothing to do with this.

TOWNSPERSON. Let us see the papers!

MRS. VERLASSEN. See it for yourselves. *(Townspeople scramble to pick their own slip of paper off the ground. We can hear people reading off Ida's name as they read their papers. She's right.)*

TOWNSPEOPLE. *(Several townspeople say the following lines.)* … Lady's right!

… They all say Ida Verlassen!

… Where's my name?!

BOXKEEPER. Sir, I swear it was in there -

TOWNSPERSON. *(Shoves the Boxkeeper.)* So where is it now?!

BOXKEEPER. *(Panicking.)* Hey, hey, I wasn't the last

person to have the box!

TOWNSPERSON. Sure! And Ida Verlassen isn't the only name in the box!

BOXKEEPER. It was Pastor Emmett! He was the last person to have the box!

TOWNSPERSON. How dare you accuse Pastor Emmett!

TOWNSWOMAN. It's a miracle! She has truly been chosen. No one else is worthy.

TOWNSPERSON. Whoever did it better explain themselves! *(The crowd once again bursts into a frenzy of conversation. Debates break out about who people think is behind Ida's name being in the box. Amidst the chaos, Ida enters the stage, returning from the prison.)*

TOWNSWOMAN. *(Approaching Ida; in awe.)* God has chosen you.

IDA. *(Nervously looking for her mother.)* Mom?!

TOWNSWOMAN. Only you are worthy.

IDA. Mom?!

MRS. VERLASSEN. *(Coming to Ida's side along with Drunk.)* Ida!

DRUNK. *(To the Townswoman.)* Leave the girl alone.

TOWNSWOMAN. I just want to be in her presence.

DRUNK. Leave her alone! *(Townswoman hurries away.)*

IDA. *(Regarding Drunk.)* Who is this?

MRS. VERLASSEN. *(Ignoring her question.)* Ida, are you alright?

TOWNSPEOPLE. *(Shouting.)* Who wants to bet that her mother rigged the drawing?! *(Some Townspeople shout in agreement. Others mumble, confused.)*

… Then why is her mom withdrawing her name?

IDA. Has this entire town gone mad?!

MRS. VERLASSEN. Ida, maybe we should go home.

IDA. No. I'm waiting for Pastor Emmett to return. I have so many questions.

MRS. VERLASSEN. What questions?

IDA. *(In a hushed tone.)* Mom, the prisoner knows me.

MRS. VERLASSEN. What did he say to you?

IDA. *(Beat.)* How did you know the prisoner is a man?

MRS. VERLASSEN. …

IDA. Mom?

MRS. VERLASSEN. …

IDA. What are you not telling me?

MRS. VERLASSEN. *(To Drunk.)* I can't do this.

DRUNK. Ida -

IDA. Who are you?

DRUNK. The answer to your questions.

IDA. …

DRUNK. Ida … your father … he's alive.

IDA. …

DRUNK. You met him today.

IDA. No. No. That couldn't have been him. Mom. Tell him he's wrong. Dad is dead.

MRS. VERLASSEN. … *(She tries to speak. Words don't come to her. She finally breaks down into tears.)*

IDA. *(To Drunk.)* What did you say to her?

DRUNK. Only the truth.

IDA. And how do you know what the truth is?

DRUNK. I lived it.

IDA. Did you know him?

DRUNK. No one knew him. We only thought we did.

IDA. You know that's not what I'm asking.

DRUNK. Yes. I knew him.

IDA. How?

DRUNK. I was part of the town patrol.

IDA. Then you're lying. They all died. Pastor Emmett said no one survived.

DRUNK. I barely did.

IDA. You're depraved. Lying to a widow about her husband. Lying to a girl about her father.

MRS. VERLASSEN. He's not lying. He's looking after you, Ida.

IDA. Then how did you do it?

DRUNK. …?

IDA. How are you the only one who made it out alive? And why did no one else know that there was a survivor?

DRUNK. Your father. He - (*A commotion. Townspeople are shouting and demanding answers once again. Pastor Emmett has returned. He walks to the center of the town square. The crowd falls silent. The clock tower chimes.*)

PASTOR EMMETT. It is time.

> *Vignette. Everyone on stage freezes except for Ida. Lighting transition to James as he enters. The clock tower continues to chime.*

JAMES. I know why you wear yellow. You're scared. I'm scared too. It's been a long time since I could honestly say that. But I still remember it so clearly. I was walking out of the front door. The sky was an hourglass. Each star a grain of sand, counting away my time. Even then, I didn't know how little of it I had left. You were supposed to be in bed. But there you were. Following right behind me. Dressed in your little yellow nightgown.

IDA. I asked you where you were going.

JAMES. You always were so curious.

IDA. You said you had to go to work.

JAMES. And I would be right back. I knew I was lying. But

that lie was all I had, and I needed to leave you with something. I should've told you the truth. You deserved that. Remember how tightly you held onto me when I hugged you that last time? I like to think that it was because you knew I wasn't coming back.

IDA. I didn't want to be left alone in the dark.

JAMES. You never did like the dark.

IDA. I was scared.

JAMES. I remember looking at you, the yellow nightgown lighting up your face. You didn't deserve to have such fearful eyes in such a happy color. I told you that from now on, you'll never be scared in yellow.

IDA. I couldn't help but smile.

JAMES. I told you to go back to bed and I would see you in the morning. I kissed you goodbye. And I left.

IDA. I waited every morning by the front door.

JAMES. I've spent many mornings in this prison wishing to see you again.

IDA. And I never saw you again.

> *End Vignette. Lighting transition back to the town scene as everyone on stage resumes their action where they left off.*

PASTOR EMMETT. In a few moments, the condemned will be brought before us. Do we have any last bets?

TOWNSPERSON: What about the new Executioner?

PASTOR EMMETT. New Executioner?

TOWNSPEOPLE. *(Confusion as townspeople say the following lines.)* … The girl's mother is withdrawing her name.

… Why is it only her name in the box?

PASTOR EMMETT. I can assure you all that Mrs. Verlassen will not be … *(Notices Drunk among the crowd.)* My god. You're alive. *(The town follows Pastor Emmett's gaze. There's a collective gasp. A survivor. Suddenly, no one is concerned about the box. Pastor Emmett walks over to the Drunk.)*

DRUNK. Pastor.

PASTOR EMMETT. *(Disbelief.)* Matthew. *(Beat; quietly.)* Is it true? You have Henry's note?

DRUNK. How do you know about that?

PASTOR EMMETT. *(A knowing look.)* Matthew …

DRUNK. *(Hesitates.)* Perhaps.

PASTOR EMMETT. All I want is an answer. That's all I've ever wanted.

DRUNK. If I let you see it … you have to choose another Executioner.

PASTOR EMMETT. You're using my son's final words to bargain with me?

DRUNK. I'm protecting the last of this town's innocence.

PASTOR EMMETT. You haven't changed.

DRUNK. Neither have you.

PASTOR EMMETT. Maybe I should introduce you to the town, hm? *(To the crowd.)* Brothers and sisters, a survivor from our town's Patrol has been among us this Execution Day. *(The town falls silent. They're shocked. A moment goes by. Someone breaks the silence.)*

TOWNSPEOPLE. *(Several townspeople say the following lines.)* … What happened to my husband?

… Did anyone else make it out?

… My brother? What did they do with his body?

PASTOR EMMETT. *(To Drunk.)* I'm not the only one looking for answers. *(Addresses the crowd again.)* Brothers and sisters, Matthew has a note written by one of our fallen. Would everyone like to hear before we bring out the condemned? *(Townspeople all let out shouts of "yes".)* Matthew, why don't you and our Executioner join me up here? *(Drunk reluctantly joins Pastor Emmett. Ida follows.)*

MRS. VERLASSEN. No! I withdrew her name.

PASTOR EMMETT. And who did you draw to replace her?

MRS. VERLASSEN. *(Flustered.)* I … it was only -

PASTOR EMMETT. Ida.

MRS. VERLASSEN. It was you?

PASTOR EMMETT. I'm only a man being obedient to God. *(To Ida.)* This is what you're meant to do.

IDA. I know.

DRUNK. Ida, think.

IDA. I have. My father is dead. He was killed by The Guard. The prisoner is the one who killed him. So I will kill the prisoner.

DRUNK. Please, think -

PASTOR EMMETT. Mathew. The note. *(The townspeople collectively cry out, asking Drunk to read the note.)*

DRUNK. *(To Pastor Emmett.)* This isn't what you think it's going to be. *(He reaches into his pocket and pulls out a small, tattered piece of paper.)* Are you sure?

PASTOR EMMETT. Read it.

DRUNK. *(Projecting his voice for the town to hear.)* "All my friends are dead. Only my enemies live." Signed Henry Emmett.

PASTOR EMMETT. *(Emotions ready to erupt.)* That's it?

DRUNK. *(Hands the note to Pastor Emmett.)* That's it.

PASTOR EMMETT. *(He reads the note. He reads it again. And again.)* How did you make it out?

DRUNK. Don't do this.

PASTOR EMMETT. Why are you here while Henry is dead?

DRUNK. It shouldn't be this way. I know.

TOWNSPERSON. Pastor, it's thirty past the hour.

PASTOR EMMETT. So it is. *(To Drunk.)* This isn't over.

TOWNSPEOPLE. *(Townspeople say the following lines.)*
... Bring out the condemned!

... I came here to see an execution!

PASTOR EMMETT. Very well. Bring out the guillotine! *(The town cheers and checks their bets with the bookies. The guillotine is rolled out. It's placed behind where they all stand.)* Bring out the prisoner! *(The town's cheers grow louder. A path is made as a guard brings James into the town square. There's a burlap sack over his head. He's brought to where the guillotine has been placed.)* Brothers and sisters, the time has come. We now are blessed to send a soul home, to its eternity ... wherever that may be. For years, our home was plagued with war. With death. With sorrow. We are the chosen few who get to live on the other side of that suffering. So it is our responsibility, our divine duty, to bring justice to those who caused that pain and suffering. *(He removes the burlap sack from James' head.)*

MRS. VERLASSEN. *(Noticing who it is.)* James! Ida, don't do this. Don't -

PASTOR EMMETT. *(Talking loudly over Mrs. Verlassen.)* This man. This member of The Guard. *(The town reacts to the mere mention of The Guard. Pastor Emmett silences them with a hand gesture.)* Plotted against our brothers. Our fathers. *(Beat.)* Our sons. It is now time for him to face his punishment. James Verlassen, do you rebuke your ways of treachery? Do you repent of your sins against our town?

JAMES. I do. I do. *(To Ida.)* I'm sorry.

PASTOR EMMETT. Do you seek forgiveness from those you have hurt?

JAMES. Yes. I do. *(To Ida.)* Ida. Please. Forgive me.

IDA. You killed my father. I'll never forgive you.

PASTOR EMMETT. Brothers and sisters, do we forgive this man? *(The town shouts with mixed responses. He holds the rope of the guillotine out to Ida.)* It's time.

DRUNK. Ida, you don't have to do this.

IDA. *(Taking the rope from Pastor Emmett.)* I want to do this.

DRUNK. *(He grabs Ida's arm that is holding the rope.)* No. You don't.

IDA. "Every time someone is executed, justice is served, and love is satisfied."

DRUNK. But there is no satisfaction in vengeance. There is only guilt. Guilt that will consume you. Every part of you. Don't do this.

IDA. *(To James; coldly.)* Do you have any last words?

JAMES. I'm sorry. This was my greatest mistake.

IDA. This is for my father - *(She goes to release the rope. Drunk tightens his grip on her.)*

DRUNK. Ida, no. I can't let you do this. Taking someone's life will change you.

IDA. What do you know about taking a life?

DRUNK. I know that it won't fill the hole that is inside of you. It won't mend your wounds. It will only infect and spread through you. It changes you, Ida. I'm the reason why this man is shackled in a guillotine, and I can barely live with myself because of it.

IDA. …

DRUNK. He betrayed me. He sent me away to die. But he came back to make it right. All of my men were dead. I was the only one alive. I was going to take my life. That's when James Verlassen showed back up one night. Still dressed in that uniform of deep red and gold. I thought he was there to finish the job and kill me himself. But he let me go. Neither of us knew that the camp was only hours away from being liberated. I'm alive because of him. He was captured by the men who came to free the camp. All to spare my life. Ida, spare your father.

IDA. This man is not my father.

DRUNK. Please don't do this.

IDA. It's what he deserves.

PASTOR EMMETT. You abandoned my son's body?

IDA. Take your hand off of me.

DRUNK. Ida …

IDA. Take your hand off of me! *(The town is growing restless. Blood needs to be spilled. Soon.)*

DRUNK. Let me do it.

IDA. …

DRUNK. Give me the rope. I'll pull it. He will die for his sins. Justice will be served. Love will be satisfied. But his blood will not be on your hands.

IDA. …

DRUNK. Please.

IDA. …

DRUNK. Ida … please.

IDA. No. *(She releases her grip on the rope. The blade falls, killing James instantly. Mrs. Verlassen lets out a scream that is drowned out by the cheers of the townspeople. Pastor Emmett leads the Townspeople in a final ritual celebration as they all exit. Ida observes the scene a moment in shock and then exits.)*

    End of scene.

EPILOGUE

"ALL MY FRIENDS ARE DEAD"

The stage is in shambles. Barely recognizable from the opening. There are empty bottles strewn about. Slips of paper litter the ground. Drunk stares in disbelief, cradling what is left in his bottle of White Label. He's laughing. He's crying. He's taking sips from the bottle to console himself. He nearly chokes on those sips as he takes them. As he approaches the base of the guillotine, he collapses in front of it. He takes another swig. He looks at the ground and fishes Henry Emmet's small and tattered note out of the mess.

DRUNK. All my friends are dead.

END OF PLAY

NOTES
(Use this space to make notes for your production)

BOBBY IS DEAD
by Marty Matfess

2M, 3W, COMEDY

Chris has been madly in love with his best friend Annie for years, but she's only been interested in dating everyone else but him. After Annie's recent break up with her boyfriend Bobby, Chris feels this may finally be what he needs to find his way into her heart, but just like that ... she's already moved on to another guy she met at a coffee shop. Being the good friend that he is, Chris has agreed to hang out with the new guy's visiting sister while they go out on a date. Oh, and let's not forget about Bobby. Turns out he's not taking the break up too well and Chris is now caught between an aggressive ex-boyfriend while having to keep new guy's sister company. A play about love, lust, and getting shot in the head.

HUGO SAVES CHRISTMAS…IN MAY!
by Steven Hayet

1M, 3W, COMEDY

For Maya Kaplan, Christmas is her life… and she hates every minute of it. As acting manager of a year-round Christmas store, Maya is force-fed jolly, subjected to hearing the same holiday songs on loop day after day. Fortunately, Maya's nightmare will be coming to an end in a few months as the store will finally shutter its doors to become a Starbucks. Or will it? Enter Hugo McGee, a longtime customer devastated to learn of the store's closing. Refusing to allow a local intuition to disappear, Hugo makes it his mission to raise the money and keep Yuletide Cheer open, despite Maya's objections.

KINGDUMB
by Jonathan Cook
10M, 6W, COMEDY

There's a new King in the land that has initiated a mysterious new tax on the citizens. Outraged, the region's finest Clock fixer, aka "Time Repair Specialist", recruits some of the most unlikely rebels to help him develop a plan to overthrow the King. Their plotting takes them on a comedic journey through perilous mountain tops all the way to the palace itself where they confront this vile King face to face. Kingdumb is a medieval fantasy comedy full of absurdist humor and illogical behavior.

BETWEEN DOG AND WOLF
by Cris Eli Blak
2M, 1W, DRAMA
WINNER OF THE 2024 CHARLES M. GRETCHELL NEW PLAY AWARD
High school friends Blake, Patrick, and Mara reunite at a hotel the day before their 10-year reunion. Forever traumatized by the school shooting that took place their junior year, the three try and fail to relive painful memories and heal broken friendships.

THE DESTINATION
by Ryan Kaminski
2M, 3W, HORROR

In the midst of a blizzard, a group of strangers seek refuge in a secluded motel, unaware that the motel proprietor and a mysterious stranger will make them part of a deadly game. A psychological horror play set during the holiday season.

www.ingramcontent.com/pod-product-compliance
Lightning Source LLC
Chambersburg PA
CBHW071359200726

48294CB00004B/1221